For Catherine Clinton

Presidents' Day
Text copyright © 2008 by Anne Rockwell
Illustrations copyright © 2008 by Lizzy Rockwell
Manufactured in China.

For information address HarperCollins Children's Books, a division of HarperCollins Publishers,
1350 Avenue of the Americas, New York, NY 10019.
www.harpercollinschildrens.com

Library of Congress Cataloging-in-Publication Data
Rockwell, Anne F.   Presidents' Day / by Anne Rockwell ; pictures by Lizzy Rockwell.— 1st ed.
p.   cm.   Summary: Mrs. Madoff's class learns about Presidents' Day and puts on a
play about the men who inspired the holiday, particularly those featured on Mount Rushmore.
ISBN-10: 0-06-050194-4 (trade bdg.) — ISBN-13: 978-0-06-050194-5 (trade bdg.)
ISBN-10: 0-06-050195-2 (lib. bdg.) — ISBN-13: 978-0-06-050195-2 (lib. bdg.)
[1. Presidents' Day—Fiction. 2. Schools—Fiction.] I. Rockwell, Lizzy, ill. II. Title.
PZ7.R5943Pre 2008   2006000345
[E]—dc22   CIP
AC

Typography by Stephanie Bart-Horvath
1 2 3 4 5 6 7 8 9 10
❖
First Edition

PRESIDENTS' DAY

E PLURIBUS UNUM

BY ANNE ROCKWELL

PICTURES BY LIZZY ROCKWELL

HarperCollins Publishers

Presidents' Day is when we celebrate the birthdays
of George Washington and Abraham Lincoln.
They were both born in February many years ago.
They were both very great presidents of our country—
the United States of America.

Grown-ups vote every four years
to choose the president of the United States.
Each person votes for the person
he or she believes will make the best leader.
They don't all agree,
so whoever gets the most votes becomes president.

We decided to put on a Presidents' Day assembly program, telling the rest of our school some things we learned about some of our presidents.

We worked hard getting ready—
painting and cutting, stirring and cooking flour paste,
and tearing strips of newspaper for papier-mâché.

Sam, Evan, Sarah, and Michiko wore
the mountain of papier-mâché we made.
"Hello, everybody! We are Mount Rushmore,"
they said all together.
"The faces of Presidents George Washington,
Thomas Jefferson, Theodore Roosevelt,
and Abraham Lincoln are carved sixty feet high
on our hard granite cliff. Now each of these
presidents will tell you about himself."

I was George Washington.
That's because my birthday is the same as his.
I was born on February twenty-second six years ago,
but George Washington was born
more than two hundred years ago.

"Good morning," I said in a deep voice.
"I led the American people when they fought
to be free from the king of England.

We won, so I was elected the first president
of a brand-new country called the United
States of America."

Abraham Lincoln was very, very tall,
and Charlie is the tallest kid in our class.

"I am the sixteenth president of the United States," he said.
"I kept the United States together when it split in two.
I said, 'A house divided against itself cannot stand,'
and I meant it.
We fought a long war to keep our nation together.
That's why it's called the United States of America.
'United' means 'many stick together like one.'"

Nicholas is a good writer who can always think
of just the right word.
When he came onstage wearing a red wig
with a short pigtail in back,
he just sat at a desk, writing with a pen made of a feather.
Everyone waited patiently while he scowled
and scratched his head, crumpled pieces of paper,
and tossed them into the wastebasket.

Finally he cried out, "At last! It's done!"

He stood up, bowed to the audience, and said,

"Good morning. My name is Thomas Jefferson,

third president of the United States.

I wrote something called the Declaration of Independence

that told why we wanted to be free from England.

Um—it's pretty good, if I do say so myself!"

He started to read what he wrote, but suddenly—

Jessica came galloping out on a hobbyhorse.

"Good morning!" she shouted.

"My name is Theodore Roosevelt,

but you can call me Teddy.

I'm the twenty-sixth president of the United States.

When I was a kid, I was sick a lot and couldn't go out to play.

But when I grew up, I was healthy and strong

and loved the outdoors.

I wanted a lot of this big, beautiful land

to always be wild.

That's why we set aside more land

to be national parks where plants and animals

could always be wild."

Pablo and Eveline came out onstage
carrying the long mural we had painted

Old Faithful spouting, and animals in the Everglades.

EVERGLADES

OLD FAITHFUL

The rest of us joined them—Mount Rushmore,
George Washington, Abraham Lincoln,
Thomas Jefferson, and Teddy Roosevelt on his horse.

We bowed while everyone in the audience clapped
for a long time.

Back in the classroom we had an election.

Everyone wrote the name of someone who'd

make a good leader on a piece of paper.

I wrote Pablo's name because he's smart and never mean.

We put each piece of paper in a box.

Mrs. Madoff counted the votes.

The person whose name appeared most often

would win the election.

Guess what? I won—just like George Washington,
Thomas Jefferson, Abraham Lincoln, Teddy Roosevelt,
and today's president of the United States!
Now I'm the president of Mrs. Madoff's class.
When I grow up, I want to be the first woman president
of the United States of America.
Wouldn't that be great?
After all, I have the same birthday as George Washington!

George Washington

1789–1797

No political party

Birthplace: Virginia

Born: February 22, 1732

Died: December 14, 1799

Thomas Jefferson

1801–1809

Democratic-Republican

Birthplace: Virginia

Born: April 13, 1743

Died: July 4, 1826

Abraham Lincoln

1861–1865

Republican

Birthplace: Kentucky

Born: February 12, 1809

Died: April 15, 1865

Theodore Roosevelt

1901–1909

Republican

Birthplace: New York

Born: October 27, 1858

Died: January 6, 1919